Story

Duke David Doub

Art:

Marchioness Sarah Elkins - Issues 1 & 2

Vizcondesa Irene Koh - Issue 3

Colors & Flashback Art

Countess Danielle Alexis St. Pierre - Issues 1 & 2

Vizcondesa Joamette Gil & Caitlin Like - Issue 3

Letters:

Vizcondesa Joamette Gil

Front Cover

Sir Tony Parker - Issue 1

Sir Terry Pavlet - Issues 2 & 3

I SAID THIS IS RUBBISH! FIX IT POST-HASTE!
...YES, SIRRAH...

SORRY, AWFUL RUDE OF ME. YOU WERE SAYING?
WELL, I'VE BEEN WRITING THE COLUMN FOR THREE YEARS NOW....
EDITOR

...AND I THOUGHT, PERCHANCE, I COULD DO SOME REAL REPORTING.

OHOOHOO-HOO...

THERE IS NO REASON TO BE RUDE, SIR.
KLINK

AH, I WAS LOOKING FOR A REPORTER WITH ENOUGH PLUCK TO LOOK INTO THE LORD HARWOOD MURDERS.
LORD HARWOOD?
LORD HARWOOD, APPARENTLY, HAS GONE QUITE MAD AND IS HUNTING PEOPLE AS IF THEY WERE ANIMALS IN THE JUNGLE.

OH MY.
SO, I WANT YOU TO INTERVIEW HIM IN THE CHOKEY.

SO, YOU WANT ME TO INTERVIEW A MASS MURDERER?
PRECISELY. HE'S IN THE PRECINCT IN HOXTON.
MOST ASSUREDLY, MISS!
THEN I SHOULD GET STARTED RIGHT AWAY?

THANK YOU GOOD SIR.
PLEASURE IS ALL MINE, MISS.

I MEAN REALLY.

I SAID NO ONE IS GONNA BE TALKING TO LORD HARWOOD TODAY.
IF YEW BLOODY WELL WANT TO TALK TO HIM THAT BAD, I KANNA ALWAYS PUT YEW LOT IN A CELL, TOO!
MA'AM.
SIR.
...WHEW..

TWAS A YOUNG LADY OF RYDE...

...WHOSE SHOE-STRINGS WERE SELDOM UNTIED.
LET ME GO!!

GUH!!!
OH!!
THWACK!

ARE YOU ALL RIGHT FAIR LADY?
I'M ALRIGHT, BUT THANK YOU.

LORD HARWOOD, I PRESUME?
DESPITE YOUR BEST EFFORTS TO HAVE VARIOUS CREATURES TEAR SAID FLESH FROM YOUR BONES.
IN THE FLESH, MY DELICATE FLOWER.

WELL, I'M HENRIETTA TILNEY FROM THE LONDON POST, AND I WAS HOPING TO INTERVIEW YOU SIR.
SEE DR. PLUM, WE'RE FAMOUS!
YES, FAMOUS FOR BEING MASS MURDERERS.
AH, BUT THAT'S NOT TRUE, MY LOVELY SWAN! WE ARE INNOCENT!
OF COURSE, FOR IT IS A TALE OF TERROR, TREACHERY, AND MURDER!
INNOCENT? PERHAPS YOU SHOULD START AT THE BEGINNING THEN?
I THINK IT'S TIME FOR YOUR MEDICINE LORD HARWOOD.

SEVERAL NIGHTS AGO, WE WERE AT AN EVENT TO CELEBRATE ME BEING NAMED HUNTER OF THE CENTURY....
Hunter of the Century
...HMM? NO CLEVER RETORT ABOUT THAT CHARLES?
ANY SUCH RETORT IS PRETTY SELF-EVIDENT.
ANYWAY, EVERYTHING WAS GOING SWIMMINGLY, BUT EVEN THEN MY KEEN SENSES COULD TELL SOMETHING WAS AMISS.
BUT NOT EVEN A SEASONED VETERAN LIKE MYSELF WAS PREPARED FOR THE DARK MAGICS THAT ASSAILED US.

BY SHEER FORCE OF WILL I WAS ABLE TO ESCAPE MY UNNATURAL SLUMBER, BUT SADLY IT WAS TOO LATE.
BUT IT WAS OBVIOUS THAT THE AWARD WAS A RUSE.
AN INNOCENT GIRL HAD BEEN SACRIFICED FOR THIS MOST NEFARIOUS OF PLOTS.
AND THEN, OF COURSE, THE BOBBIES ARRIVED AND ACCUSED ME OF THE HORRIBLE SLAYINGS AROUND LONDON. A MOST MASTERFUL TRAP TO ENSNARE ME.

I BELIEVE YOU.
NOT TO WORRY. I HAVE AN IDEA.
BUT WHO'S GOING TO HELP YOU?
GOOD SIR, I'M A VERY CAPABLE WOMAN. NO NEED TO WORRY.
I LIKE THAT GIRL'S SPIRIT. I HOPE SHE CAN HELP US.
MAKES NO DIFFERENCE. I HAVE A PLAN OF MY OWN.
OH?
NO. I WOULDN'T WANT TO RUIN THE SURPRISE.

WHAT!
SEE HERE, WHAT IS GOING ON?
AND HOW DID THE MOB KNOW WE'RE HERE? ...PROBABLY JUST READ THE PAPER.
THE MOBS ARE GETTING RESTLESS. SO WE HAVE TO MOVE YOU LOT.
DOESN'T LOOK LIKE YOUR YOUNG REPORTER FRIEND IS GOING TO BE ABLE TO SAVE US IN TIME.
WHERE IS HENRIETTA? I NEED TO BUY HER SOME TIME.
NO BEOWULF.
NO. BEOWULF.

TRUST ME, I'M SAVING YOU FROM A LOT OF HURT.
31

3177

HMM, LOOKS LIKE WE'LL HAVE TO GET CAPTURED AGAIN SO MISS TILNEY CAN HELP US.
...
HAPPY TO OBLIGE.
SHLACK
STOP.
AND DROP IT, SIR.
shink
..SIGH...

HOLD IT RIGHT THERE, GOOD SIR! THESE ARE FREE MEN.
AH...YES...LET THEM GO, INSPECTOR.
IF THE JUDGE SAYS YOU'RE FREE, THEN YOU'RE FREE.
MY HENRIETTA, YOU ARE QUITE CUNNING. LIKE A SUPPLE TIGRESS, YOU ARE.
I HAVE TO LET THEM GO, OR SHE'LL PUBLISH ABOUT ME AND THE CHOIR.
FINE THEN.
WHAT?
AHEM.
TWEEEEEEEEET

IT'S THE KILLER! LORD HARWOOD!
OI, THERE HE IS!

SLUM
IT SEEMS THEY JUST WANT YOU, BEOWULF.
OH NO.
BLOODY HELL.
WE'VE BEEN HAD.
HMM.
DONT WORRY, CHAPS, I'VE GOT THIS.

FOR THE QUEEN!

HOLD YOUR BREATH, MISS TILNEY.

HACK, COUGH..
Kliishh

BLAAARGH!!
HUUUURGH!!!

WHAT DID YOU DO EXACTLY?
OH, JUST THREW SOME IPECAC GAS AT THE CROWD.
BUT YOU GOT LORD HARWOOD, TOO.
BLEEECK...
AND NOW HE'S SAFE FROM A PUMMELING BY THE MOB.

YOU'LL HAVE TO FORGIVE DR. PLUM'S DEMEANOR. HE'S ACTUALLY MY OLDEST AND DEAREST FRIEND.
I GUESS ONE CAN BECOME DISTANT SEEING THE SAD SIGHTS A DOCTOR SEES.

WELL, I'M SORRY TO HAVE DRAGGED YOU INTO THIS, MISS TILNEY, BUT I'M GLAD YOU HAVE FAITH IN US.
WELL, I WILL ADMIT THAT YOUR STORY IS QUITE FANTASTICAL, BUT I HAVE A GOOD READ ON SUCH MATTERS.

I SUGGEST YOU STAY AT HARWOOD MANOR. JUST UNTIL SOME OF THE EXCITEMENT HAS SETTLED DOWN.
THERE ARE QUITE A FEW QUESTIONS I DO WANT TO ASK YOU.

WELL THEN! WELCOME TO MY HUMBLE ABODE.
MIND YOU, I CAN ONLY STAY SO LONG. IT WOULD BE IMPROPER FOR A LADY TO STAY TOO LATE.
BUT OF COURSE, I PERFECTLY UNDERSTAND MY DEAR.

GOODNESS!
WATER TO CALM YOUR NERVES?
PLEASE HAVE A SEAT.
THANK YOU, MY DEAR.
YES...QUITE A COLLECTION YOU HAVE.

EXCUSE ME A MOMENT.
JUST A MOMENT.
BUT SIR!
shirk
shirk

THE YOUNG MISS!
DR. PLUM!!!

GRUNCH GRUNCH SLASH SLASH

klick

klick

BAA-BOOOOM!

RAAAAARGH!!!!
KRRRRAAGGH!
BAA-BOOOOM!
klick
PILLOCK!!

DONT JUST STAND THERE WITH MOUTH AGAPE, BEOWULF, GET MY BAG ALREADY!
RIGHT, RIGHT!

THE
HARROWING HAPPENSTANCES
OF LORD HARWOOD.

Part 146

In the Grand Palace of His Highness Sri Sir Chamaraja Wadiyar, Knight Grand Commander, Maharaja of Mysore, everything was a blur of activity as they prepared for the wedding of the Maharaja's eldest daughter, Princess Jayalakshmi Ammani. Everyone was excited by the upcoming nuptials because everyone loved the Princess Ammani. Not only was she greatly adored for her beauty, but she was admired for her wit and wisdom. It was only natural that the happiest day in her life would be a joyous occasion for all of the people of Mysore.

But where was the Princess? Yes, the Maharaja's palace was quite spacious. It would be quite easy to lose a person in the army of servants preparing for the lavish wedding, but the Princess's brightness would be easy to spot even in a monsoon.

So, quietly but ever so efficiently, the Maharaja's most loyal guards were sent about the grounds of the palace in search of the fair Princess.

In the oldest of the Hindu temples on the palace grounds, one such guard searched. He was filled with reverence as he entered and thought perhaps the dutiful Princess may have come to offer her silent prayers before the wedding ceremony.

But what welcomed the guard was haunting and ominous indeed. There were sharp echoes of wails and groans filling the air of the most holy temple. There was a great calamity of heavy thuds, as if flesh was being pounded against the stone in the most violent of manners.

In his heart of hearts, the guard was truly frightened by this most supernatural happening. But for the sake of his duty to the Maharaja and the Princess, he pressed forward to see what this otherworldly occurrence was.

The guard froze in his tracks, shocked to his core by what he saw.

Naked! Hairy! Sweaty! Fornication!

Atop the fair and most beautiful Princess, the darling of all the land, was a fat British chap grunting and rutting away. They were clothed in only the skin they were blessed with at birth.

Only because the clumsy oaf slipped on the pristine form of the Princess did he happen to notice the guard standing behind him, still aghast at the sight he cannot unsee.

With an experienced air, the Englishman was quickly off the ravished Princess and was running past the guard. At this point the Guard realized his duty and he was quickly after this foul foreigner. The guard's sword was held high, as he shouted for his sworn brothers to aid him in the chase most dire.

Despite his small stature and his gross girth, the Englishman was quite adept at avoiding his enraged pursuers. But sheer numbers can easily outweigh skill and luck, and the Englishmen soon found himself trapped.

He found himself cornered in the middle of the wedding ceremony, waiting on the most precious bride. But what they found was the British man who robbed their Princess of her most sacred virtue. The Englishman took it as a point of pride that everyone's attention was so sturdily locked on him. He even took a moment to pose as if he were a Greek statue, right before the guards piled on him with unbridled hate.

The British fellow was dragged up to the Maharaja, who was patiently waiting for his glorious daughter to begin a new chapter in her life. As the entire wedding party watched with amazement, the guard who had found the Princess and the Englishmen whispered the saddest of news to the Maharaja. Grief filled the Maharaja's face as the horror fully set its hooks into his soul.

Without hesitation, the Maharaja ordered several of the guards to hold this foul beast down on all fours, like the creature that he is. Then the Maharaja quickly pulled one of the guard's swords from its scabbard, and raised it high, ready to give the British bastard his chop. Seeing the all too familiar shadow of a blade, the Englishman knew that the next few seconds counted quite dearly.

With practiced ease, the Englishman rolled hard to one side, dragging some of his captors with him. This in turn caused them to collide with the rest of the men holding down the Briton and creating a heap of men that the Englishman deftly crawled out of.

A sharp strike of metal against stone sent sparks flying at the Englishman as the Maharaja barely missed cleaving deep into the man's lumpy flesh. Another swing of cold steel swung past the Englishman, as he clambered to his feet and started to haphazardly flee from the rigorous strokes of the Maharaja's sword.

Various ornate antiques and relics were strewn to and fro from the desperate attempts of the Englishman to slow his vigorous pursuers, but the guards and the Maharaja simply swatted them aside with angry slashes of their blades. Theirs was a righteous anger, and nothing on the mortal realm was going to stop them from seeing justice done. Quite a commotion had begun to stir through the wedding party from the surprise arrival of the Englishman. Servants and guests were running back and forth, talking in the loudest of tones. Amidst this chaos, no one even noticed the Princess's entrance into the morass. How would anyone think that this tussled-haired strumpet, clad only in a silk curtain, was the people's same sweet and demure Princess? So, of course, her cries of leniency toward her lover fell on deaf ears.

As the Englishman flew through the hall of the palace, his hand caught something heavy and hard. He pulled mightily, sending the unseen object flying to ground with a heavy thud. The impact of the brazier on the ground forced its contents to go flying about, scattering hot ash and embers all over the room. Naturally the hall was full of the most delicate of fineries, which also happened to be quite flammable.

With the swirling chaos of the chase and the realization that the oh-so-special Princess had become a woman this day in a manner no one dared anticipate, no one really noticed the fire that had started until the flames were licking them in the face. Panic gripped everyone. Old friends and family trampled each other in merciless attempts to escape the blazing furnace that the grand place had become. All loyalties and familial ties were all tossed aside, as each person bravely rescued their own neck.

During this, the once revered Princess was all but forgotten, pushed, shoved and beaten by the crowd until she was trapped in a small nook of the grand hall, clutching her knees to her chest, wondering what would become of her. When out of nowhere, a strong hand pulled the young, frightened princess out of the flames and the despair. The Englishman firmly led her by the hand through the grasping tendrils of the giant blaze that the once marvelous Palace had become.

After the dizzying sprint through her home, she found herself led to one of the third floor balconies of the palace. She looked back at the hungry flames, all too eager to cook her alive.

"We're trapped. I will burn for my sins," she said, tears welling in her beautiful eyes.

The Englishman put an arm around her slender waist and said, "You just need to have faith my dear." And with that he jumped with her over the balcony and into the crystal clear pool below. As they came up for air, the Englishman couldn't help but admire the

sight of the cool water sliding down her gentle curves.

But he also noticed the sadness in her eyes, so he pulled her close and said, "Fear not my lovely bird, for tonight is but the start of your life, and I'm sure it will always be as exciting as a fierce creature like you deserves." And he punctuated his comment with a kiss so passionate that it set a fire in her loins that easily dwarfed the fire devouring the mighty palace behind them. With that kiss, the Englishman ran off into the night, leaving her to bask in the glow of the one giant flame that was a mere tribute to the love that they had shared.

~~~

Meanwhile across town, there was intensity and action of the cerebral sort, occurring in a seemingly unassuming hotel suite. Formulas, computations and precise measurement were beingconsumed by an obsessive mind, directed only at his goal of science.Beakers, vials and every other container imaginable were being used to discover the truth. What truth you may ask? The TRUTH. The science, the reason behind it all. Doctor Charles Plum was a fervent devotee of the church of logic and order. He devoted many of his waking hours to the study of this.

But on this fine mid-morning, he found himself rather distracted from his research.
~~~

Light.

Light pouring in from the window of his suite. Didn't he close those curtains? No, he didn't, because it was unnecessary to do so in the dark of night. Surely he should have foreseen that his studies would have taken this long. No, if he could have deduced how long it would take, then he would have known what the results would be and how to understand that data, thereby knowing the answer immediately, instead of taking the insufferable amount of time it takes to arrive at the conclusion.

Finally, the annoyance got to the Doctor and he marched to the window to close the accursed curtains, when a peculiar sight greeted him at the window. The Palace of Mysore was on fire. Engulfed in flames. More than likely to be nothing but cinder and ash come nightfall. Curious, but none of Doctor Plum's concern, he still had plenty of research to do.

Naturally, just as he sat down at his desk to begin adjusting and manipulating his precise instruments, his door flew open and he found himself staring at a heavyset man, wearing nothing but a turban on his head and small wrap of silk covering his *undercarriage*.

"No matter how many different ways you show up, I'm not going to ask what you've been up to," the Doctor said as he continued to concentrate on his work.

Paying no heed to the Doctor's words, Lord Beowulf Harwood began to hastily pack up the Doctor's belongings, which only served to irritate the normally patient Doctor.

He gripped Lord Harwood firmly by the arm and said, "What exactly do you think you are doing Beowulf?"

Lord Harwood easily shrugged off the Doctor's touch and resumed packing, "Sorry Charles, don't have much time to explain, but we're going on a hunting expedition."

The Doctor regained his calm and reached out for his tincture of water and powder from the cocoa plant. "Fine, you've got me to ask it Lord Harwood. What have you been up to?" he asked, after taking a sip of his water.

Instead of responding, Lord Harwood tried to dodge the question by packing more of the Doctor's things, but the good Lord chose poorly. The Doctor's ire was definitely raised, but he calmly moved to impede Harwood's progress. The Doctor didn't speak or act, but his displeasure was very clear. Actually, it was very dark. The light seemed to flee the room in terror. Clouds loomed over the hotel. The hotel's occupants could feel their hearts slow and their throats tighten from the Doctor's malice overflowing.

But a warm smile weathered it all. Lord Harwood just gave his charming smirk and bowed apologetically.

"Sorry good chap. Forgot how sensitive you can be," Harwood said, "But I've been in spectacular form today, and we really do need to go."

Just as suddenly as the anger appeared, it just as quickly went back into its lair. The Doctor simply nodded and began to pack his equipment.

~~~

A particularly busy street of Mysore was not in its usual character. All the vendors, people and traffic had ceased. Everyone had fled. Doors shut, windows shuttered. The blood flow of this usually vibrant street had dried up.

The reason was marching down the street. At the head of a large force of very tense men, all ready to draw their swords in the service of duty, his Highness Sri Sir Chamaraja Wadiyar, Knight Grand Commander, Maharaja of Mysore was looking for repayment for the insult done onto his house, his honor, and his daughter. And there was the man he was looking for. Nay, that foul miscreant was a demon clad in the skin of man. The Maharaja must act, not only for himself but for all other fathers out there. No daughter would be safe unless the sexual beast was banished from this plane.

There at the end of the street was that same demon, attempting to beat a hasty retreat. Lord Harwood and Doctor Plum were loading up their cart, desperate to escape the righteous grasp of the Maharaja. Lord Harwood immediately noticed his impending doom looming at the end other end of the street. So, of course his industrial spirit came to life to expedite the loading of the cart and his necessary departure.

The Doctor could not help but notice Lord Harwood's rapid breathing and increased sweating. "Is that what we're running from Beowulf?" inquired the Doctor.

"Ah yes, he's the father of the bride," Lord Harwood simply replied as he continued to exert himself to load the cart.

"The bride? White does seem to have a physiological effect on you. Well, let me have a polite chat with the gentleman," Doctor Plum said. He began to walk toward the wall of wrath that was about to wash over them.

Lord Harwood looked concerned as he watched the Doctor walk forward to face the
~~~

music. "Our last conversation was pretty lively, so I really wouldn't press the man further," Lord Harwood tried to caution, but the Doctor was not paying heed.

The Doctor had no inclination of discussing anything with the Maharaja. The Doctor simply pulled an innocuous-looking vial from his pocket and threw it onto the ground, before the wave of wrath crested and came crashing down on him.

A quiet *crack* was all the vial made as it hit the ground. The liquid inside vaporized instantly. Quickly, it expanded into a large ominous cloud that enveloped the Maharaja and his men. The gas weaseled its way into their mouths and nostrils, and down into the recesses of their lungs. As the mixture of chemicals began to corrupt the blood and body, painful changes began to erupt in the Maharaja and his men. Lord Harwood finished packing and paid no attention to Maharaja and his soldiers' suffering even as they writhed on the ground in torment.

"Thank you for that Doctor, I'm just about done loading things up," and he nodded his head at the Doctor.

"Small solutions for small people. Simple enough Harwood," replied the Doctor, climbing onto the bench of the cart.

Soon enough, the duo were on their way, leaving their pursuers in the dust.

~~~

Night had set once the Maharaja and his loyal servants were able to gather their wits. Their precious bodily fluids were mostly spent on the ground, thanks to the Doctor's noxious gas. But the Maharaja wasn't discouraged. Of course, the devil had a fiendish sorcerer at his command. This was a grand task given to him by the gods to go forth and do good. From the ashes of his despair would come a great victory for him and his people. His commanding voice issued forth into the air and stirred the souls of his sworn soldiers. The soldiers understood what needed to be done. They picked themselves up and dusted off. They were stronger of arm and lighter of spirit. They would march forth and get this Englishman, this plight on the Earth. They would go through the circles of Hell if necessary to hunt him down. They would chase him into darkest recesses of the nether realms.

They marched forward with their Maharaja at the lead, but quickly enough their procession was stopped. Standing before them was the Princess Jayalakshmi Ammani resplendent in her beauty, but there was something much deeper about her. There was a new quality to her that seemed to be the final piece to puzzle. She was complete. She was whole.

"Father, you are not going any farther. You shall not harm that man. Despite his rough exterior he is a very good soul," the Princess said with authority.

But the Maharaja was still the man of power, and he knew he was right. "Dearest Daughter, please step aside. I understand you're filled with foolish notions of love and affection for this Englishman, but it rings false. Let your father set things right," he said as he tried to move past his precious daughter.

But the Princess wouldn't let her revered father pass. She blocked his progress and said, "No Father, you are the one who is mistaken. I'm actually hurt you think so little of me and my decisions. But then that's why I did what I did. I'm not a little girl anymore. I'm a woman and worthy of your full respect. But I realized you would never listen to your baby, so I had to take drastic action. When I met the Englishman and heard his honey-drenched words, I knew he would be perfect. He was the one who made me a woman, but it was my choice, my step to take."
~~~

The full weight of the Princess's words settled on the Maharaja. His shoulders stooped and he looked down at the ground dejectedly. Time drifted slowly, as the tension seemed to have it in a tight grip. It was so still and quiet that people emerged from their homes and other streets, coming to see what this hole in the world was.

With eyes full of tears, the Maharaja lifted his head and looked at the Princess, directly into her shimmering eyes. "I am so sorry you had to go so far to get my attention. I thought I was totally attentive to your needs, but I realize the error of my ways. I was merely seeing in you what I wanted to see, not what was truly there," he said as he reached out to her.

Despite all of the Princess's newfound strength and power, she still crumpled at her father's acceptance. She rushed into his arms, and both of their tears flowed freely. Their bodies trembled with joy. All of the people around - the soldiers and the common folk - began to cry as well. Many not really understanding what was happening, but their hearts were moved by the moment nonetheless. It was a very poignant day in Mysore.

Elsewhere, in a little cart going through the dense foliage surrounding the city of Mysore, Lord Beowulf Harwood was thinking of Princess Jayalakshmi Ammani. He was thinking of the tryst they had shared. He was thinking of her thick, black tresses. Her smooth shoulders. Her firm, rounded breasts. Her....well we could go on, but we have a profound respect for a woman's innate innocence and do not wish to speak further in such a crass manner.

END

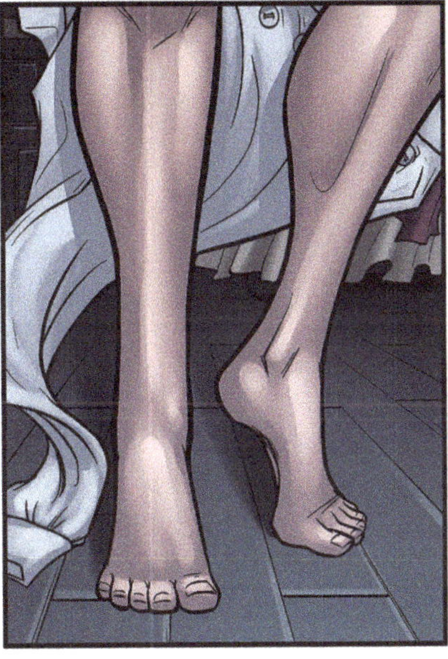

Calon lan yn llawn daioni...
Techach yw na'r lili dlos...

Does ond Calon....eh?

KRAASPLASH

SLASH

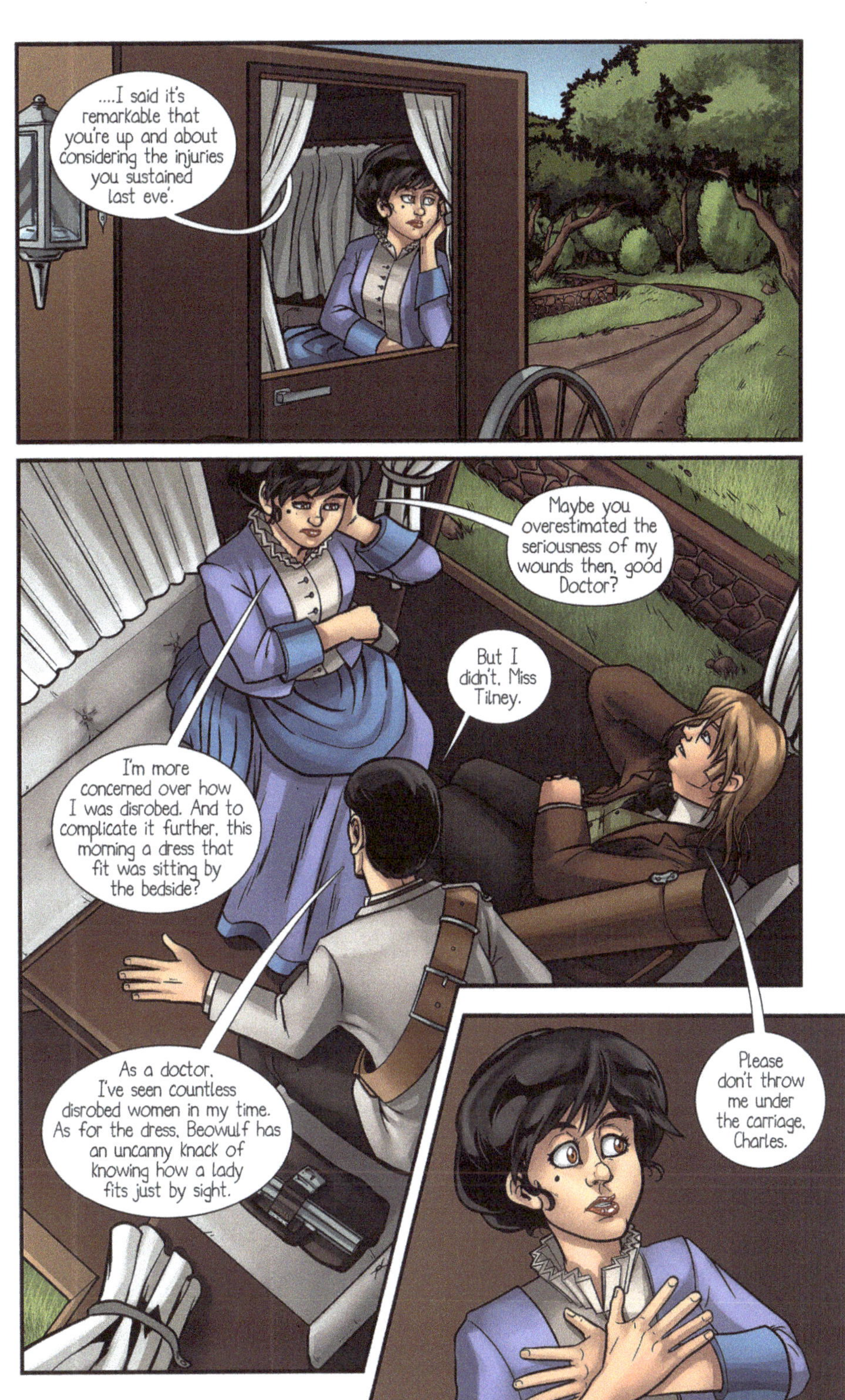
....I said it's remarkable that you're up and about considering the injuries you sustained last eve'.

Maybe you overestimated the seriousness of my wounds then, good Doctor?

But I didn't, Miss Tilney.

I'm more concerned over how I was disrobed. And to complicate it further, this morning a dress that fit was sitting by the bedside?

As a doctor, I've seen countless disrobed women in my time. As for the dress, Beowulf has an uncanny knack of knowing how a lady fits just by sight.

Please don't throw me under the carriage, Charles.

And this was the manor you were taken to a fortnight ago?
Base trickery I tell you.

Hmmm, let us take a look around then.
Seems to be locked, but I'll fix it soon enough.
Please sir, if you'll allow me.
KLACK
KLACK
KLACK

CLICK
KLACK

Tch, you have to be impressed with her.
No, I do not.

You are distracting me.
But you just started.
You are in my light.
Come Miss Tilney, let us look about outside.

मैंने तारों को देखा बहुत दूर जतिना मैं उनसे
whoooooosh
वे दिखै इस पल मेंटमिटमिाते अतीत के पल
अँधेरे की असीमता में,सुबह का पीछा करती रात मेंयह तीसरा पहर

Here, let me help you ma'am.
Thank you, sir.

Lord Harwood? My hand?
Oh, pardon.
Ah, thank you for the handsome dress by the way.
A dress is just thread and fabric until your beauty brings it to life.

I know I may seem like an utter cad at times, but I'd like to say that I do have a lot of redeeming qualities.
I'm sure you do, Lord Harwood.

I fancy...
I see someone watching us. Get Dr. Plum. You should be able to catch them.
I'll stay here and keep an eye on them.

Come Charles, the hounds are loose, the hunt is on!
Yes, ma'am.
Mmmmm, of course they are.

I thought we were supposed to call you "The Wolf"?
That woman really packs my bore, Charles. She may actually be able to tame the rampaging rhino.
Just waxing with a dash of poetic license, good sir.

...oh my....

He tripped and took a nasty tumble.

I saw him stumble against a stone and down he went.
Of course he did, dear.

I say a good thrashing will set this man's tongue a'waggin.
Don't be so gauche. I'm a doctor and can't abide another man being injured.
My way is much more humane.

And sticking folks with various tonics and tinctures is humane?
Now, why don't you be a good chap and speak up.
Yes.
If you don't explain, various fates may befall you....
...and none of them will be pleasant.
Ald Nick! Don't keel me.
Best to start at the beginning where most things tend to start.

I don't know the play, but apparently they had no understudy, so they were in a bit of a pinch. Since I did some acting as a lad,
I was more than happy to oblige.
It was a simple but pivotal role, so I was quite pleased with my performance. You didn't suspect a thing.
So about your daughters then?
I have no daughters, sir.
Of course.
So, what more do you know about this event then?
Not much more. I was paid by the foreign chap and I left posthaste.
Foreign you say? Get a good gander at him then?
No sir. I did not.

Do you at least know where this theatre troop resides?
Yes ma'am, they operate out of the Old Vic.

So to the Old Vic then. I assume one of you knows where it is.
Just a moment Charles. Henrietta?
I'll be along in just a moment.
Just wanted to apologize to the poor soul for the scare I'm sure we gave him.
Quite.
Ah, you are a blessed angel who extends her kindness to all.

Remember, I have your scent now, so I can find you at my convenience.
I suggest you run along now.

I don't want to interfere, but I would have given that man a good tongue lashing.
Huff...
Huff...
Ah, but Lord Harwood, I'm a writer. I have a way with words. My point was made quite clear to the gentleman, I assure you.
THRASHTHRASHTHRASHTHRA
I told them everything...
Bloody... huff... hell...
I told them everything...
MOTHER OF GOD!!

ROYAL VICTORIA HALL

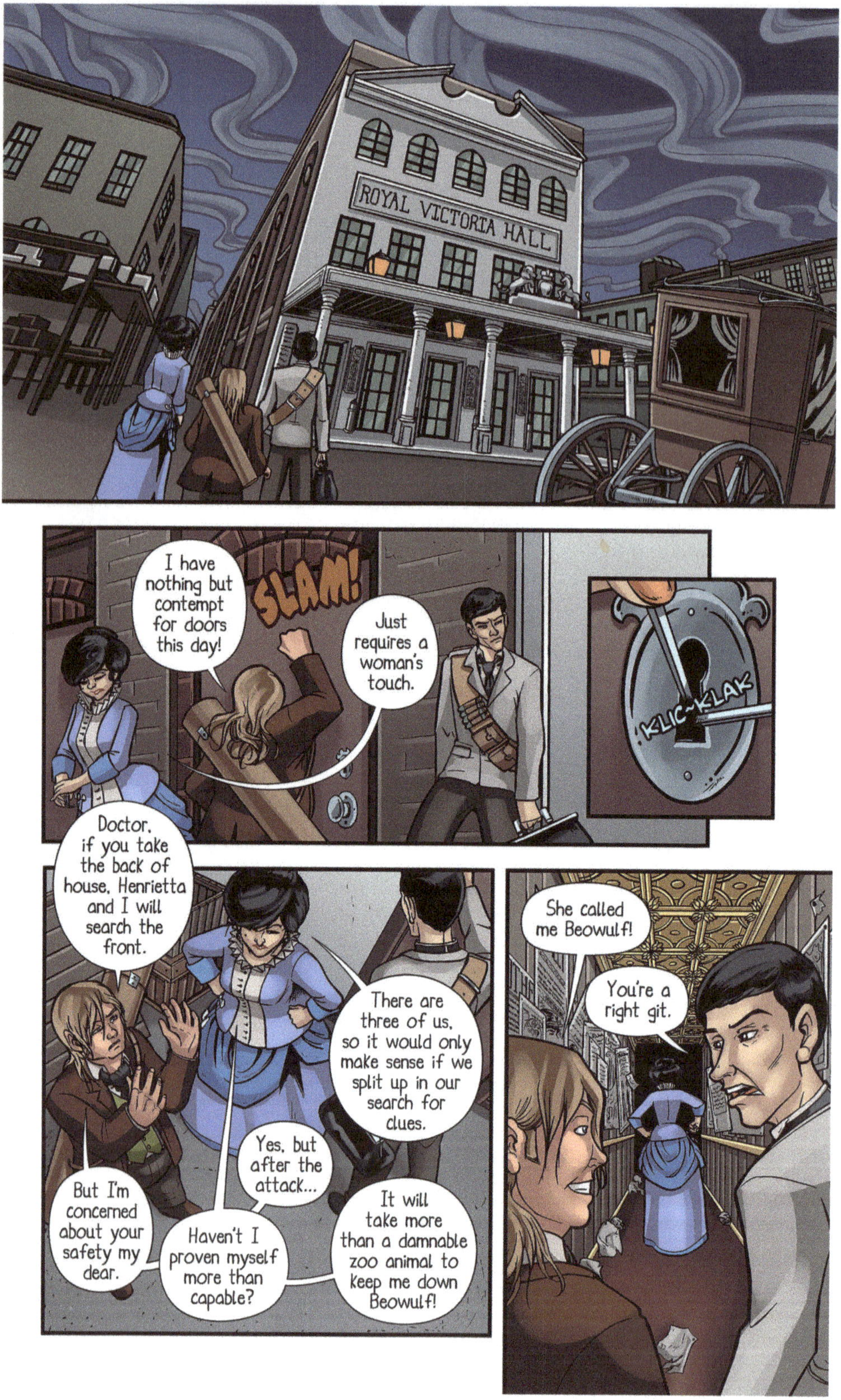

I have nothing but contempt for doors this day!
SLAM!
Just requires a woman's touch.
KLIC~KLAK

Doctor, if you take the back of house, Henrietta and I will search the front.
There are three of us, so it would only make sense if we split up in our search for clues.
But I'm concerned about your safety my dear.
Haven't I proven myself more than capable?
Yes, but after the attack...
It will take more than a damnable zoo animal to keep me down Beowulf!

She called me Beowulf!
You're a right git.

Bloody hell.

Oh.

Ahem.

And perished, all along of love for me!
Oh, now, indeed, I feel, as 'tis my duty.
That I have been the Beast, and he the Beauty!

Oh, were he but alive again...
to pop....
the question...
I would have him in a....
Is it a bargain?

Hmm, this blood seems fresh.

Would you really wed The Beast, if I could prove he wasn't dead?
Oh lord!
Harwood, would you please stop this tomfoolery!

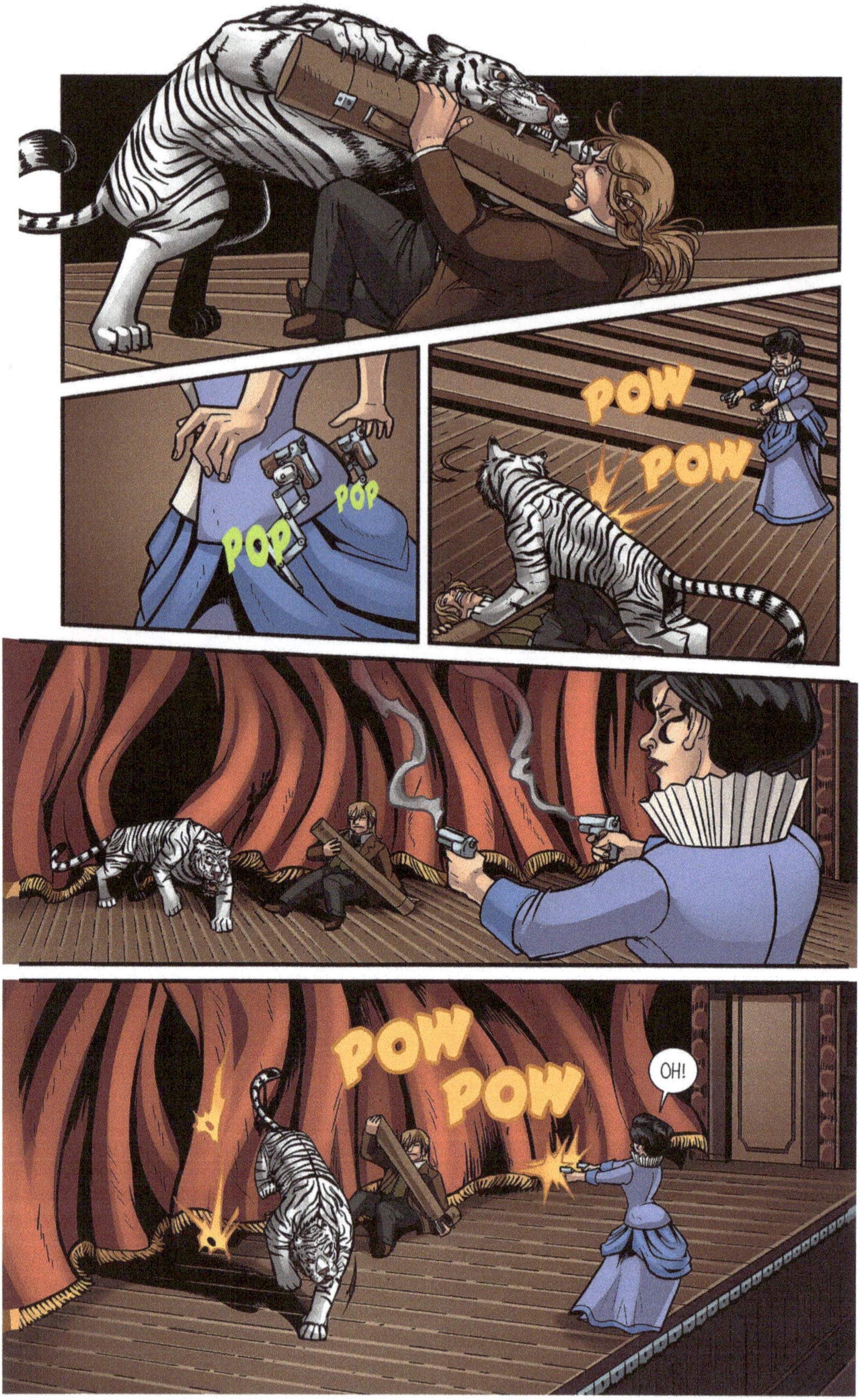

POP
POP
POW
POW

POW
POW

POW
POW
OH!

Hell and damnation.
AAAAAAEEEI!
BAA-BOOOM!!

Are you okay, Henrietta?
Luckily, my corset took the brunt of the fall.
SHHHHRACKRASH
PRICK

Uhmf!

Didn't make the solution strong enough.
Did you actually use us as bait?
Yes.

TWEEEEEEEET

Oi, there!
Stop!
I guess he didn't see the large white tiger running about London.

THE HARROWING HAPPENSTANCES OF LORD HARWOOD

Part 147

With a strong steady swing, the blade of the Talwar ended the greenery's life with brutal quickness. Muscles strained and the skin was slick with moisture as the blade was swung over and over again, in an attempt to assert dominance over the lush foliage. A lesser man would have been worn down by the jungle's defiance, but Lord Harwood was not a lesser man. He persevered with a strength almost supernatural in its fierce effectiveness. Once where there was dense growth for several generations of man, there was now a path torn through it all, as if Lord Harwood made it by sheer will alone.

Behind this great man, this man of amazing efficiency, was a train of servants suitable to a man of Lord Beowulf Harwood's stature. A multitude of paid locals struggled to carry the burden steerage upon their backs. When these hired hands first took this job, they thought their pockets would be easily lined with coin. When their eyes beheld the doughy physique of Lord Harwood, they wrongly assumed his fortitude would not last in the inhospitable jungle. Laboring slavishly for the third day, the locals realized there was more to this Englishman than meets the eye.

Unaware of his men's unspoken complaints, Lord Harwood continued his grueling task of making the tangle passable for men. Up and down his arm would go.

Up. Down. Up...

WAIT! His arm froze in mid-swing before his mind could understand the sudden stop. There was a man in the foliage. He was curiously studying one particular plant out of the multitude of leafy life surrounding them.

"Plume, what in tarnation are you doing," asked Harwood as he could now feel the exhaustion spreading across his body.

"Currently I'm ignoring your annoying habit to steal from colonial vernacular," replied the Doctor as he continued to devote his full attention on the plant before him.

Being of a curious nature, Lord Harwood knelt next to Doctor Plume to examine the plant closer. But no matter how he tilted his head, left or

right, the importance of the plant didn't seem to rise at all.

"Charles, I don't get it," as Harwood scratched his head in confusion.

"Ricinus communis, castor oil plant," the Doctor simply replied as he carefully exacted samples into a vial. "This may be the most poisonous plant to exist. It has the power of death over man, so I want to study it," continued the doctor as he carefully put the vial up.

"You're such a caring and thoughtful chap, Doctor," says Harwood as he stood up.

"I just don't like such control over mortality with something unthinking. If I can understand its power then I have the control," replied the Doctor as he stood up and was careful to brush off any dust or detritus.

Lord Harwood just let the words wash over him and gave it a simple shrug in unknowing acknowledgement. The good Lord was about to say something to change the subject but with his keen eyesight he spied something that would change the subject for him. He froze in place, every muscle tense but unmoving. He gestured to Doctor Plume to do the same and he complies wordlessly.

The Lord's uncanny vision spied his prey deeper into the jungle. The Doctor moved silently back to quiet the caravan as Lord Harwood began to stalk his quarry undisturbed. Despite his lumpy size, the Lord manages to weave his movements amongst the foliage with the greatest of ease. It was almost like he was possessed by the spirit of a great jungle cat, and in fact that's what he would often whisper in a lady's ear before he would gently bite it.

As Lord Harwood continued to pursue his game, large droplets of water begin to fall in such a downpour to be able to pierce the dense canopy of the jungle growth. Everything became slick and it became almost dark as night as the clouds blotted out the sun. But this deterred Lord Harwood not one iota. The mud threatened to pull him under and he could barely make out the silhouette of his prey, but he pressed on despite it.

Actually he pressed on because of the challenge of it all. He was positive he saw the fabled White Elephant and he would be the one to hunt it down and possess it. With his mighty skills and famed cunning, this mythical creature would be brought low by his hand. The thrill of anticipation caused his heart to pump faster, his blood to flow more quickly, but he still maintained composure. He was not about to loose the White Elephant because of a foolish mistake on his part. It would be a fair contest between man and beast.

Lord Harwood had to get dangerously close to get a good aim on the White Elephant. And he noticed something wrong. He felt something wrong. He lowered his gun and decided to approach the beast even closer, risking life and limb if the beast trampled or gored him. And nothing happened.

That's when he noticed the stench.

The stench of death.

A flash of lighting finally illuminated what Lord Harwood had already deduced. The White Elephant was already dead. Mauled and caked in dried blood. Flesh already rotten. The carcass was oddly propped up against a large rock, so at a distance it would seem to still be standing, still filled with life.

Lord Harwood started to wonder why someone would do that, but the answer interrupted his train of thought. From behind, he heard the screams of his attendants. It was screams of suffering. Lord Harwood ran back toward the sounds of pain as hard as his legs could push his squat frame. As he ran into the fray, one of his men ran past him in terror. The man was clutching his stomach in a desperate attempt to keep his entrails more inside than out. One would think the man would have been prone on the ground with such a grievous wound, but the look in his eyes told you that the fear would not let this man stop his flight.

More concerned with the fight, Lord Harwood let the man pass. Lord Harwood moved into the scene of battle and oh what a sight it was. The tangy smell of iron filled the air as his men ran around in maddening disarray. If they weren't running about all panicked, it's because they lay on their ground as their precious life blood mixed with the soil.

Hunched over one such victim, Doctor Plume was covered in a man's humors, working hard to keep the man from slipping off this mortal coil.

"Charles," simply prompted Harwood as he stood over doctor and patient.

"You didn't get a white elephant Beowulf. You got a bloody white tiger," replied Plume as his patient slipped through his tight medical grasp.

"A WHITE TIGER! MARVELOUS! Simply Marvelous," exclaimed Harwood, and the hunt had truly begun.

Harwood did a quick inventory of the situation and it all added to danger. Typically a tiger would pick off the weakest, the lone stragglers, but this one went straight to the bulk of the herd. To the heart of the group. Harwood had to respect this beast's stones, but it was killing his men and that was something he couldn't abide.

Suddenly there was sharp quick scream and then there was a furious rustle of undergrowth as the tiger attacked another man. Harwood ran hard to spot but the man was dead and the tiger was gone. Then there was another scream and another fleeing native was brought low by the hunting tiger. Harwood again tried to track the White Tiger, to get a bearing on it but the creature was too swift and too stealthy.

Harwood had enough of this deadly game. He was going to take control of the sport once more. Harwood stood on a large rock and let a rifle shot ring out for all to hear.

Everything stood still and quite for a moment and Harwood shouted with his full strength, "You show wits devil tiger, but do you have courage? I am the only prey worthy of you, you predacious pussy! Have at me!"

And with that proclamation Harwood ran deeper into the jungle, heedless of the consequences. Doctor Plume took the cue and started to direct the healthy to gather up the wounded.

"All right you uneducated viral vessels. If you're ambulatory, helps those who can't," and then the Doctor started to walk in a seemingly random direction.

"Were you go Dokor?" asked one of the frightened natives.
"We're going down to the river. It's a more defensible position," the Doctor replied without stopping or turning around.

The natives struggled to keep up with the Doctor. There are more harmed than not, so they had to work hard to just limp along but the Doctor kept his same cruel pace.

While gloom hung over the Doctor Plume and his native charges, Lord Harwood was having the time of his life. It was a literal game of cat and mouse. They would trade their roles from one moment to the next. Lord Harwood would have the deadly White Tiger dead to rights and then the White Tiger would be pouncing on the good Lord. Around and around they went like a child's top spinning and spinning. The chase just made the Lord hungry, hungry for the cat's hide. He was bound and determined to mount and stuff this feline if it was the last thing he did. But Lord Harwood didn't include the White Tiger in the discussion. The Tiger showed craftiness that defied what was capable of its ilk. Any other man would have fled from a Tiger that was so supernatural in its nature. Not Lord Harwood. He drank this like it was milk from the teat. He wasn't discouraged but encouraged by the unique talents of this solitary beast.

And the struggle went on. The monsoon's onslaught made their battle more like a rough swim in the Channel than an actual fight. Harwood noticed that his tread was treacherous and this gave him an idea. He made his way toward the cliff that overlooked the river below. Looking down he could see the Doctor leading his charges across the raging waters. Apparently some of the hired hands didn't make their journey because there were bodies being carried away by the river. Harwood gleefully waves at his friend and confidant, but he then hears a noise that tells him he dallied too long on such sentimentality. He turns around and there was the tenacious White Tiger, all it's sinews and muscles all tight and ready to lunge at Lord Beowulf Harwood.

All he could was raise his rifle and brace for the hit.

BABAM!

Off goes the shot as the Tiger's full weight slams into the mass of Lord Harwood. The unmovable object met the unstoppable force. A well place rifle stock fills the maw of the White Tiger, but a sharp snap of those same jaws turns the rifle stock into matchsticks. The White Tiger opens wide again, eager to feel Harwood's flesh grinding between its teeth, but a queer feeling came over it. It was the sudden pull of gravity once more as it and Lord Harwood fell over the edge of the precipice. The inertia of the White Tiger's dive pushes them over, so Lord Harwood's plan half worked. Falling to his death was not part of it. Sure getting the kitty wet would have been grand, but not if he has to take the plop too. Either this was going to hurt or not at all. Lord Harwood would soon see. He was having a splendid time.

END

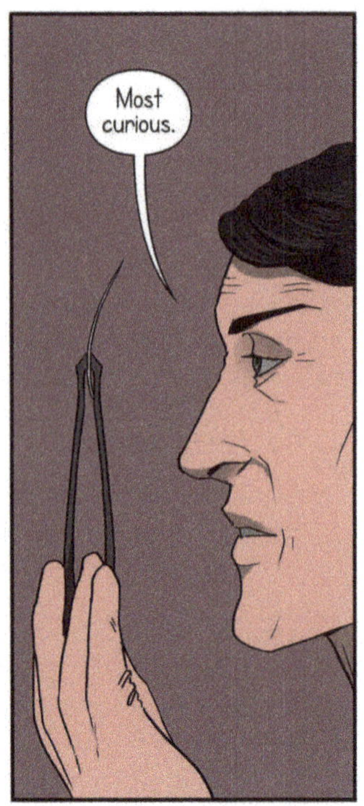

Most curious.

A picture is starting to form.

Hmm. I still enjoy being surprised.

Meanwhile in the East End...
That's a lovely pair you have, ma'am.
Excuse me?
Thank you, Mr. Seville.
You're welcome, Miss Tilney.
They're the only useful thing my mother gave me.

If my mother is to be believed, my grandfather put them to good use.
Can we get back to the matter at hand, Broderick?

Sorry sir, you know I am an admirer of fine craftsmanship.
Yes, but I need my guns looked at.
Then I must remind you of your tab.
Oh no, that's not necessary.
Please sir, it is a matter of some import.
If you wish, I can pay what he owes to expedite this.
Let me just get my tools and we can head back to Lord Harwood's manor and I'll get to work.
Ugh.
If it's no trouble.
No, no trouble at all, Miss.
Ugh.

Why are you really tagging along, Broderick?
I've noticed in the paper lately about your spot of trouble, so I thought I could help.
I'm capable of taking care of myself.
And Miss Tilney?
That's a long story.
Are you upset by my concern?
I appreciate your concern, but I'd hate to drag you into this debacle.
I feel that the risk I'm about to face is worth it.
Just as I have made my choice, I'll respect yours.
And thank you for not questioning why a mere woman is involved.
Why would gender affect your abilities or judgment?
Welcome to the cricket team Broderick! Let me explain what has happened to our intrepid hero so far!

DOCTOR! Where are you, Plum?

ARE YOU STILL SLEEPING? WAKE UP, CHARLES!

...!
What have you done, *you cad?!*
Merely testing to see if I've finally gotten the dosage right.
Explain yourself Doctor!
Plying a woman's virtue with Absinthe is one thing, but this?
This is all in everyone's best interest.
If you will allow me a moment, I can explain how this woman has become a willing, or un-willing, complication to our current problems.

"First, when I noticed that Henrietta was healing unusually well, I decided to take some samples."
"I figured the rapid recovery was due to my superior skills, but a Doctor of my caliber always double-checks his work."
"Then a series of strange clues led me to a deceased derelict who had similar wounds as Miss Tilney."
"Adding that with the sample I was able to acquire from a live specimen, the total picture became clear."

I believe the young lady has contracted a disease that--

SLAM

SMACK

Later that night in Marylebone...

Lord, there is a lady here to see you.
Let her in then.

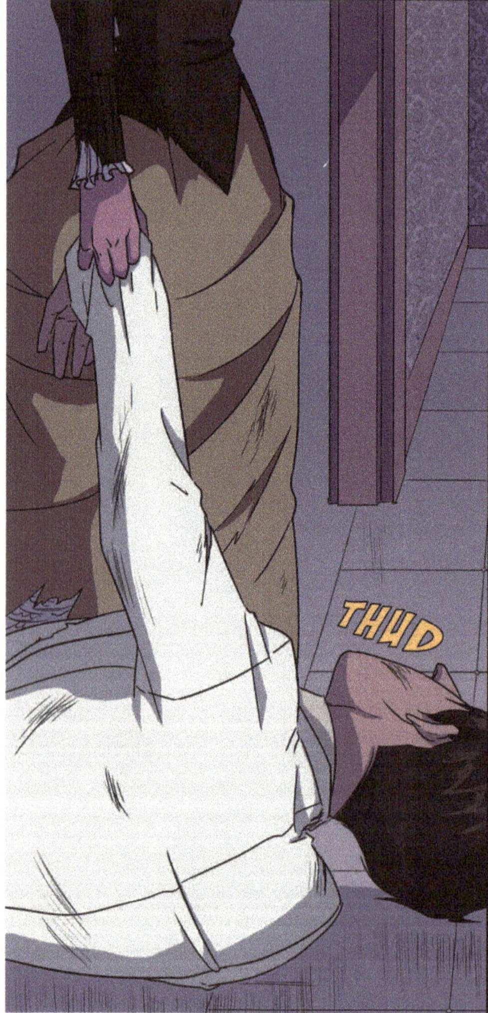

THUD

THUD

Well that's putting the cat among the pigeons.

And Lord Harwood brought low by a woman. Makes my victory that much sweeter.

Maybe I'll add insult to injury and make you my mate as well. But that is meant as an honour for you, not a punishment.

...why...
Hmm, she speaks? What was that, dear?
...why...

Yes, people should hear the story that has caused so much pain.

"Even with the British Empire marching into our home, we managed to stay hidden, as we always had."
"So when it came to time to go hunting, I felt safe leaving my mate, full with cubs, alone."
"Little did I realize that the black-hearted hunter, Lord Harwood, was on the prowl."
"I swore that the hunter would become the prey."
"I would rid the world of this monster and all he held dear."

"So, I came to the capital of your vile Kingdom, to find the worst among you. And I learned how to strike at the heart of a noble."
"I arranged Lord Harwood would lose his status and station before he lost his life."
"A noble's vanity is his weakness, so that was the bait of my trap."

But you were able to free them from my trap.
I do not hate you for that. I admire your strength and conviction.
For that, you may have the honour of killing them.

Be free...
...pater noster...

...qui es in caelis...
GRRRR

GROOOWL

POKE

NOW, Broderick NOW!
Hah, got the dosage right.

BAA-BOOOM! BOOM!

I've never killed a man before.
Well, you didn't start tonight. Look.
Mr. Seville, I need you to protect Henrietta above all else.
I will do my utmost.

Good god...
...what have they done to you, Miss Tilney?
KA 
BA
BAA-BOOOM!

KA BAAM KA BAAM
KAARAKK
I appreciate a strong woman, hence why I've rewarded her so. You sir, won't be so lucky.
We killed them, Charles!! Huzzah!
People don't turn into tigers.
I mean they're proper dead, right?

Sigh...
Broderick!?!

Escape is not an option, gentlemen.

SWOOSH
STAB STAB
STAB STAB
STAB STAB

SHHHKRASH

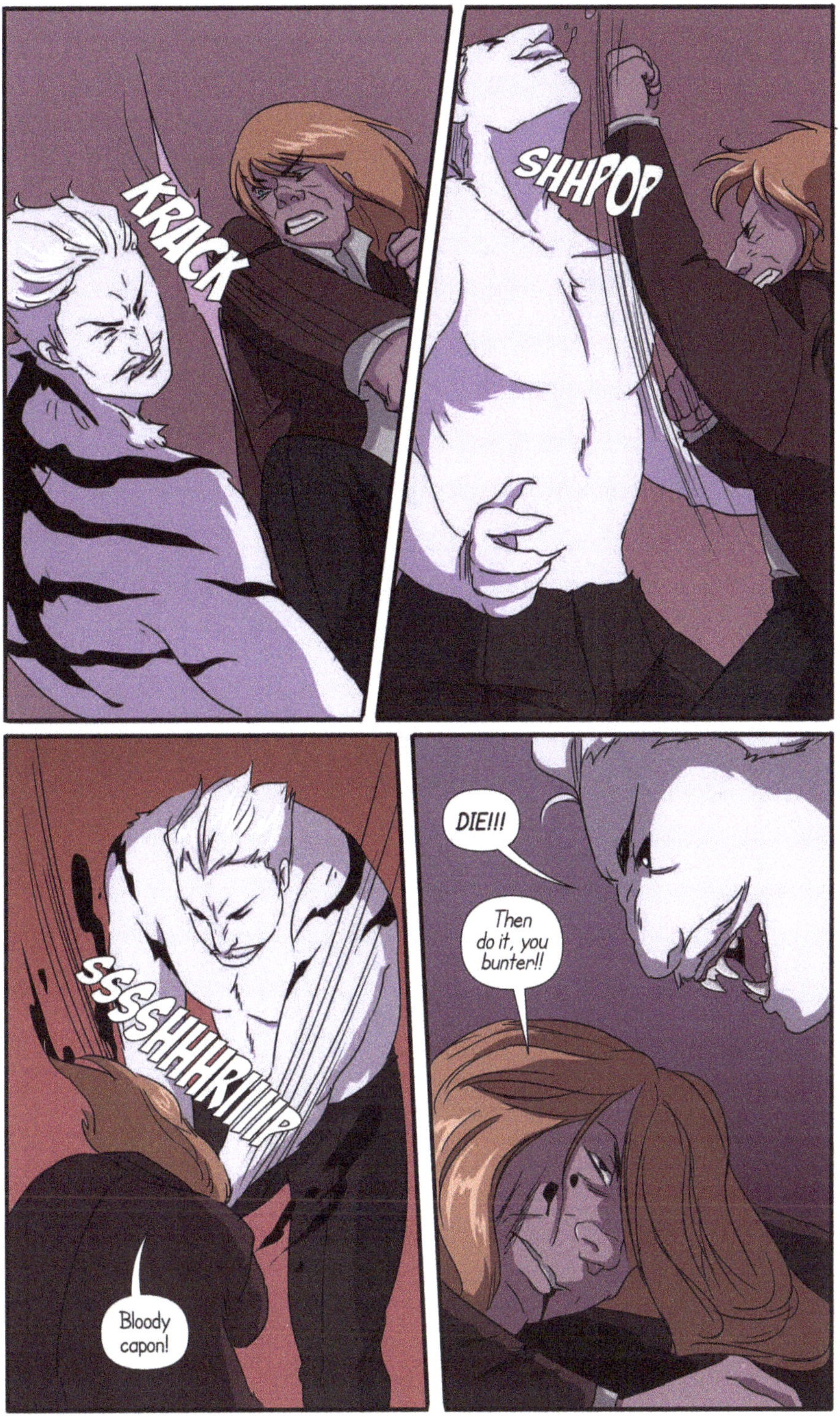

KRACK
SHHPOP

SSSHHHRIIIP
Bloody capon!

DIE!!!
Then do it, you bunter!!

Excuse me.
.....?
TAP TAP
Never keep a lady waiting.
GEYAH!
SLASH

How do you resist my grasp?
I just do.

Dr. Plum says killing you will cure me.
That's one experiment of his I'm willing to try.

....but... hurk...if...gah...I take...gasp.....my gift back!

No bother ....
THUD

SNAP
May you be eaten by a cat and the cat be eaten by the Devil.

Smashing outfit, dear... have to take you to the Pump Room in that sometime.
Bastard, made me kill twice now.
Do you ever stop, Lord Harwood?
I'm a hunter, and you are prey most worthy. Speaking of animals, would you be interested in raising a litter?
Have you seen what happened to last man who asked me that?

Point taken, ma'am.
Enough of that, we have friends to tend to.
Yes, very good friends indeed.

...And it's only a tuppence, Guv'nor!

I'll take one.
Much thanks, ma'am.

London Post
LORD HARWOOD FRAMED BY FIENDISH FOREIGNER
Written by Henrietta Tilney

And how are we doing, ma'am?
Much better, Mr. Seville.

Time for tea, isn't it?
Some tea would be marvelous.

Until next time, good reader.
There will be more ripping good action in the pages of The Trials and Tribulations of Miss Tilney.

THE HARROWING HAPPENSTANCES OF LORD HARWOOD

Part 148

The lament of the damned polluted the air with its piteous cries. Flesh violet to green, filled with puss and ooze. Pale white bones erupted up from the skin. The inner workings of man out on grisly display for all to see.

Doctor Charles Plum was practicing medicine.

I will follow that system of regimen which, according to my ability and judgment, I consider for the benefit of my patients, and abstain from whatever is deleterious and mischievous.

"So much blood," exclaimed one of the natives holding down the Doctor's thrashing patient.

The Doctor was dressed in crimson finery. His demeanor was a reflection in the scalpel that was cutting the meat of his patient.

Weak and trembling bodies stood just on the edge of the fire light with their sharpened stick. Their fear was so great that ever rustle of the forest brought visions of the White Tiger as it sunk its sharp teeth into their fleshy tissue. The tension was too much for one slip of a man and he started to run off into the dark foreboding jungle. Before he could a foot into the underbrush, a wave of disappointment hit him so hard it sent him reeling backwards. As he laid on the ground in bewilderment, the Doctor loomed over him.

"You can't leave. The others are sick and can't defend themselves. If you flee, they die," said the Doctor looking through the man.

Without responding at all, the man dragged himself to his assigned post. He had a hollow listless look in his eyes as he peered about for trouble.

Doctor Plum worked through the night. Unrelenting, never flinching. Sewing and stitching sinew. Setting and splinting bones.

Night turned into day.

It was only by the grace of the alkaloids from the coca plant floating in his water that kept the Doctor awake and alert. But even the Doctor's remarkable constitution had its limits. Fatigue began to lower its heavy curtain on the Doctor. With his remaining clear thinking, he emphasized to the poor men of India gathered around him how important it was to remain vigilant. It would take time for it to be safe to move the wounded, so this particular piece of jungle was where they would be staying for the immediate future. He made it crystal clear that if any of them failed in their vigilance, then all would be lost. Even if some of them broke rank and managed to flee from their demise, they would never escape from his wrath.

With that positive reinforcement, the Doctor felt comfortable enough as he could to consider taking a quick slumber.

Sleep, the only chance the Doctor finds escape from his incredible intellect and the problems the world taunts him to solve.

Time passes and as he awoke he found the world gave him a new riddle to unravel. He no longer lay by the river bank surrounded by his patients and hired hands. He was deep in the verdant jungle, alone. As his vision focused and he studied his surroundings, he found he was not so alone.

There was blood. Blood everywhere. Traces of it on the leaves, the branches, the brush, blood on everything.

He knew what was happening. He was being toyed with. Everyone else was dead and he was next. It was a pathetic attempt to make him afraid, to panic and give the hunter a good chase. But all the years being by Lord Harwood's side had taught Doctor Plum all about predators. Such ploys would not work with him.

He attempted to conceal his movements, but every crack of a twig, every rustle of the foliage echoed thunderously all around.

"How does my corpulent associate manage to move so deftly in the wild," muses the Doctor as he wanders about the jungle.

Suddenly the Doctor stopped because he thought he heard more

noise than just himself. But he didn't hear anything, and that was
a quandary. Plenty of expeditions with the good Lord Harwood,
taught the Doctor that there is always sounds of nature about. The
only time there isn't is when the animals know they're being stalked.

The Doctor reaches for his pistol that he carries for protection, only to
find that is was gone. His patience was at an end. The White Tiger
dragged him into the jungle without waking him, but also had the
state of mind (not to mention the manual dexterity) to have removed
his firearm? If it wasn't for the threat on his life, he would have
found the scenario preposterous.

"No this is quite absurd. Beowulf would love such a game, but I
most assuredly am not him," Doctor Plum said plain and clear for
anyone who may be listening to hear.

The response to the Doctor's words was a brief flash of the White
Tiger running about in the undergrowth. But just as quickly as the
beast was visible, it disappeared again.

The Doctor realized an encounter with the White Tiger was immi-
nent. He did a quick account of what he had on his person and found
it lacking. He was going to vent further about the nonsensicality of
his circumstances, but he didn't have the time.

He started to do inventory of the wilderness around him. What flora
and fauna was about that the he could work with? Ah yes the pan-
try was fully stocked. The Doctor busied himself with preparing his
concoction.

First the Doctor could sense the White Tiger slowly circle him as he
continued his mixture. He knew the curiosity of the White Tiger
would get the better of it, but ever the hunter it approached with
caution. Then he could smell the musk of the beast. Its flanks must
be covered in sweat from the exertion of slaughtering everyone else
in the party. He could also smell the pungent smell of iron from the
blood that was probably splashed on the white fur.

ROAR!

Suddenly, the White Tiger lunged through the foliage and seeming
had caught the Doctor unaware. With a quick reversal the Doctor
spins around at the last moment and blows a strange powder into the

fearsome face of the White Tiger.

Immediately the tiger reared back and started yelping in pain. There was extreme pain in its eyes and it couldn't see. Before it could flee, the Doctor quickly picked up a rock and slammed it down on the tiger's head. There was a satisfying crunching noise as the rock stuck meat and bone.

"Sorry, no time for precision work," the Doctor says as he raises the rock once more for the final blow.
But then with a might swipe of the claw, and the tiger's and doctor's roles were reversed again. The Doctor barely got the rock down in time to shield himself from the attack, but the force of it was still enough to knock him to the ground. The Doctor was reduced to crawling and scrambling on the jungle ground as the White Tiger was right behind him snapping away by scent alone.

SNAP.

SNAP.

The tiger then makes a leap of faith and manages to pin the Doctor to the ground. With the full weight of the monster on his back he couldn't move, he couldn't fight back. All he could do was wait for the powerful jaws of the White Tiger to grip his skull and crack it like an egg for a full breakfast.

He felt the warm splash of blood gush all over him.

He didn't feel pain though. Doctor Plum was a tad disappointed that he had apparently gone into shock.

"Let me meet the silent conqueror now," triumphantly shouted Lord Beowulf Harwood as he stabbed again at the White Tiger with his handmade spear.

But the White Tiger was aware of the danger now and managed to dodge the vicious stabs of Lord Harwood's mighty spear. The White Tiger fled blindly into the thick woods and Lord Harwood would have followed if the Doctor hadn't tackled him.

"Damn it man! I will have that tabby stuff and mounted," Lord Harwood exclaimed as he got up.

"No, we've both had enough of that queer fiend. Judging by the amount of its blood on me, it should expire soon," replied the Doctor as he tried to wipe the excess blood off his person.

"But you know as well as I this in no customary Tigris! This is a beast sent forth from Hades itself for me to test my mettle on," proclaimed Harwood as he stopped his foot like a petulant child.

"Ignoring the questions of why Beelzebub had needed to send you a trial, we are still mere mortals. And as your physician I would like to point out that if your last strike won't kill the tiger, then we will not survive another encounter," calmly explained the Doctor.

"Drats, I suppose your right Charles. Still was the most fun I've had in awhile," expressed Lord Harwood as look around for the right direction to go.

"And yes it will be the most fun the other lads will ever have," the Doctor simply stated as he followed Lord Harwood.

"Hoorah, true enough that. Won't they have tale to tell Saint Peter at the pearly gates," Lord Harwood shouted with glee.

"Actually they were all probably Hindu," clarifies Doctor Plum.

"Excellent, then maybe they'll be reincarnated again and we can do another adventure together. I hope none of them come back as a gorgeous wagtail though. Hate to roger a gal who once was a bloke. Be tad bit confusing," mused the Lord Harwood as he picked the trail out of the jungle and back to civilization.

A low cloud bank had begun to cover the Nilgiri Hills, obscuring the tallest peaks from sight. Rudra was clad in only simple trousers and had a large pack slung over his shoulders. His skin was damp from sweat as he clambered over the rocks. His bare hands and feet continuously scraping and scrambling over the rough stone. Interspersed among the outcroppings of rock where lush evergreen that was even more impassible.

But passed Rudra did because this was his home. The unseen path was for him alone to see. The unknown trail was his alone to walk.

He couldn't full enjoy it because of his form, but it was necessary to carry the pack. How he would have loved to feel the ground beneath his paws. To feel the cool wind blow across his long body. To let the assault of subtle but complex scents fill his snout.

Alas he had had to fumble around and waste time on two legs. But he'd be home and be reunited with Kavya soon enough. How his arms ache to hold her once more. He hoped the trinkets and baubles he brought her would be enough to appease her. The works of metal he found in the towns seemed to fascinate her so. To take something from the ground like that and manipulate it to into a work of art is something to be almost envious of man and its abilities.

Almost.

Living amongst the original people of India had never really been a problem. They understood and respected the old ways and knew what fear was. Both people were able to co-exist without much trouble or sacrifice for either side.

But the British?

England saw itself as master of the world. Their God given duty was to inflict their ideals of civility and law on other, lesser folk. But that was all a sham, a cover for the dark deeds that they did. It was about greed and power.

Rudra could understand power. Power was part of the natural order of things. But greed? Greed did not exist in the wild. It was a construct of man, and like most man-made objects it only truly served to benefit man.

As Rudra was lost his thoughts about the annoyance of Englishman and their boorish mindset, he didn't notice that his leg was wet with something other than his own perspiration. He finally stopped and reached down to wipe his leg.

He found blood on his fingers. He brought it to his lips for a taste.

Kavya!

Shredding the back on his back, Rudra shifts and begins to rush in a controlled panic. The unmistakable tang on his tongue was that of his mate. During his flight, he noticed slashes of red painted on the green.

He rushed into the rough hewn stone home and found her lying lifeless on the ground. He saw the deep gaping wound in her side and the broken spear near lying beside her.

Rudra feel down in tears on top the form that was his wife. He gripped her tightly like in some vain attempt to prevent her soul from fleeing him. He tried crying out her name, but his throat choked it off. All he could do was clench his eyes shut and smother his face in her bosom so he no longer had to see that horrid sight.

And that's when he smelt it.

He smelt a scent on her. He couldn't place is specifically but the general aroma was all too familiar to him.

He smelt the blood of an Englishman.

Rudra now knew what his goal in life was. He would hunt down this Englishman and destroy his world just like the Englishman took Rudra's world away.

www.ingramcontent.com/pod-product-compliance
Lightning Source LLC
Chambersburg PA
CBHW061111100726
47911CB00012B/503